KU-002-365

Favourite Christmas Stories

Brown Watson

ENGLAND

This book contains the stories THE NIGHT BEFORE
CHRISTMAS, CHRISTMAS JOYS, THE CHRISTMAS
SNOWMAN, and NONI THE CHRISTMAS REINDEER,
copyright © by Rand McNally & Company in 1950, 1980,
1977, and 1979, respectively. All rights reserved.
Printed in Czechoslovakia
50249/4

CONTENTS

The Night Before Christmas

'Twas the night before Christmas,

   when all through the house

Not a creature was stirring,

   not even a mouse;

The stockings were hung
by the chimney with care,
In hopes that St. Nicholas
soon would be there.

The children were nestled
all snug in their beds,
While visions of sugarplums
danced in their heads;

And mamma in her kerchief,
and I in my cap,
Had just settled our brains
for a long winter nap;

When out on the lawn
    there arose such a clatter,
I sprang from my bed
    to see what was the matter.

Away to the window

 I flew like a flash,

Tore open the shutters

 and threw up the sash.

The moon, on the breast

of the new-fallen snow,

Gave a lustre of midday

to objects below,

When, what to my wondering
eyes should appear,
But a miniature sleigh
and eight tiny reindeer,

With a little old driver
so lively and quick,
I knew in a moment
it must be St. Nick.

More rapid than eagles
his coursers they came,
And he whistled and shouted
and called them by name:

"Now, Dasher! now, Dancer!
now, Prancer and Vixen!

"On, Comet! on, Cupid!
on, Donner and Blitzen!

"To the top of the porch,

to the top of the wall,

Now, dash away! dash away!

dash away all!"

As dry leaves that before
the wild hurricane fly,
When they meet with an obstacle,
mount to the sky,

So up to the housetop
the coursers they flew,
With the sleigh full of toys,
and St. Nicholas, too.

And then, in a twinkling,

I heard on the roof

The prancing and pawing

of each little hoof.

As I drew in my head,

and was turning around,

Down the chimney St. Nicholas

came with a bound.

He was dressed all in fur

from his head to his foot,

And his clothes were all tarnished

with ashes and soot;

A bundle of toys

    he had flung on his back,

And he looked like a peddler

    just opening his pack.

His eyes—how they twinkled!

    his dimples—how merry!

His cheeks were like roses,

    his nose like a cherry.

His droll little mouth

    was drawn up like a bow,

And the beard on his chin

    was as white as the snow.

The stump of a pipe

he held tight in his teeth,

And the smoke it encircled

his head like a wreath.

He had a broad face

and a little round belly

That shook when he laughed

like a bowlful of jelly.

He was chubby and plump,
a right jolly old elf,
And I laughed when I saw him,
in spite of myself.

A wink of his eye
        and a twist of his head
Soon gave me to know
        I had nothing to dread.

He spoke not a word,

    but went straight to his work,

And filled all the stockings;

    then turned with a jerk,

And laying his finger
aside of his nose,
And giving a nod,
up the chimney he rose.

He sprang to his sleigh,
   to his team gave a whistle,
And away they all flew
   like the down of a thistle.
But I heard him exclaim,
   ere he drove out of sight,
"Happy Christmas to all,
   and to all a good night!"

Christmas Joys

Mr. and Mrs. Mouse named their
new baby Chris Mouse, because he
was born at Christmastime, and a
happy time it was.

"Come, let's take Chris to see the
joys of Christmas," said Father Mouse.

The first thing they saw was a snowman.

"Snow falls from the sky on cold days in winter," said Mother. "Let's make snowballs !"

Soon they were throwing
snowballs at each other, and making
a snow-mouse with holly berries for
eyes.

On the High Street, all the shop windows were alight.

"There's a crib," said Father, "like the one where Baby Jesus was born on the first Christmas, long ago."

"And there's the first mouse he saw !" said Chris.

"Oh look!" said Father Mouse. "Our house people have made a special treat for us!"

"It's really for the birds," said Mother, "but they won't mind if we have a nibble."

"That pretty ring of holly and ivy and fir reminds people that green things grow, even in winter. It's nature's gift to us," said Father.

"My, it smells good in here!" said Chris Mouse.

"Mrs. People is baking mince pies and gingerbread cookies for

tomorrow's feast," said Mother.
"There'll be turkey and stuffing . . . "
    "And lovely mouse-cheese for us,"
said Father, sniffing happily.

"What pretty paper and ribbons!" said Chris Mouse.

"The Dad and Mum people are wrapping presents," said Father Mouse.

"And Liz and David are writing cards," said Mother. "One of the joys of Christmas is remembering all your friends."

"Now they are decorating the tree," said Father. "Right on top they put a star, to remember the one that shone over Baby Jesus's stable."

"Why are the children hanging up stockings?" asked Chris Mouse.

"If they have been good children, they will find their stockings full of goodies tomorrow," said Mother.

"Listen to that beautiful sound!" said Chris Mouse.

The Mouse family ran to their outside hole.

"They are singing Christmas carols," said Father. "Carols tell of the joys of Christmas."

Suddenly there was the sound of jingle bells.

"That must be Santa !" said Mother. "He and his elves make toys for children—and mice—all over the world."

Chris Mouse hung a mouse-sized sock at the foot of his bed and tried to sleep.

Suddenly there was a *thump* on the roof. Then *whoosh* down the chimney came roly-poly Santa Claus.

Chris Mouse darted out of his
hole and up the chimney.

On the roof was a beautiful sledge,
loaded with sacks. And in front of it
were eight tiny reindeer.

Santa came puffing up the chimney. "Ho, ho!" he said. "Off we go—lots more houses to visit before morning!"

His eyes twinkled at Chris Mouse. Then he was gone, sledge, reindeer and all.

Chris Mouse was very sleepy. He slid down the chimney and snuggled deep into bed, with all the joys of Christmas dancing in his head.

"Happy Christmas!" Liz and David were shouting merrily as they opened their presents.

There was a toy train for David, with railway tracks and signals.

Liz found a wonderful robot doll
that could add numbers and play
puzzle games and talk.

Dad got a Christmas tie, all red
and green. And Mum got furry
slippers.

"And now for us," said Father Mouse.

He kissed Mother and Chris. "That's mistletoe," he said, pointing overhead. "It's good luck to kiss under the mistletoe!"

"I like it," said Mother. "Let's do it again!" And they did.

Chris Mouse stared and stared at the tiny fir-branch Christmas tree. There were ribbons and tinsels. And underneath was a lovely mouse-sledge, just right for three.

"Looks as if Santa found our little mouse house," said Father.

Just then there were happy shouts outside. Liz and David were riding their brand-new sledges down the hill.

"Come on, let's go," said Father.

"And a Merry Christmas to all!" shouted Chris Mouse.

The Christmas Snowman

SAMMY was a handsome new snowman. He had button eyes, a carrot nose, and a bowler hat. But Sammy didn't want to be an ordinary snowman. He wanted to be a *Christmas* snowman.

"A *Christmas* snowman?" said Squeaky Squirrel, as he jumped off a branch to say hello. "Now that would be something special."

"*Very* special," said Corky Crow. He swooped low, and landed on Sammy's shoulder. "But how can you be a Christmas snowman?"

"Well," said Sammy, "first I'll need some decorations. You do lots of travelling, Crow. Have you seen something I can use?"

Corky Crow thought a minute,
then took off for his favourite spot,
the dump. On a pile of rubbish he saw
a wreath that looked like new. Carry-
ing it back in his beak, he dropped it
over Sammy's head.

"Thank you," said Sammy. "This looks fine around my neck. Now what about you, Squirrel? Do you have anything I can use?"

Squeaky Squirrel thought for a minute, then scurried back to his hidey-hole in the tree. From deep inside he pulled out a big red bow he'd found on the ground.

"Here you are, Snowman," he said. He tucked the ribbon on Sammy's hat.

Fanny Field Mouse heard the commotion and poked her nose out from under a log. "A new snowman! How do you do!"

"He wants to be a *Christmas* snowman," said Squeaky. "Do you have any decorations we can use?"

Fanny thought a minute. Then she disappeared in her hole. Soon she was back with her children behind her, pushing a huge gold ball.

"It's a tree ornament," said Fanny. "The children found it last year."

"Beautiful," said Sammy, as they fastened it on his chest. "Thank you, friends. Do I look like a Christmas snowman now?"

"Oh, yes," shouted Squeaky Squirrel. "Seeing you makes me feel all happy and Christmas-y inside." He clapped his paws together and started doing somersaults.

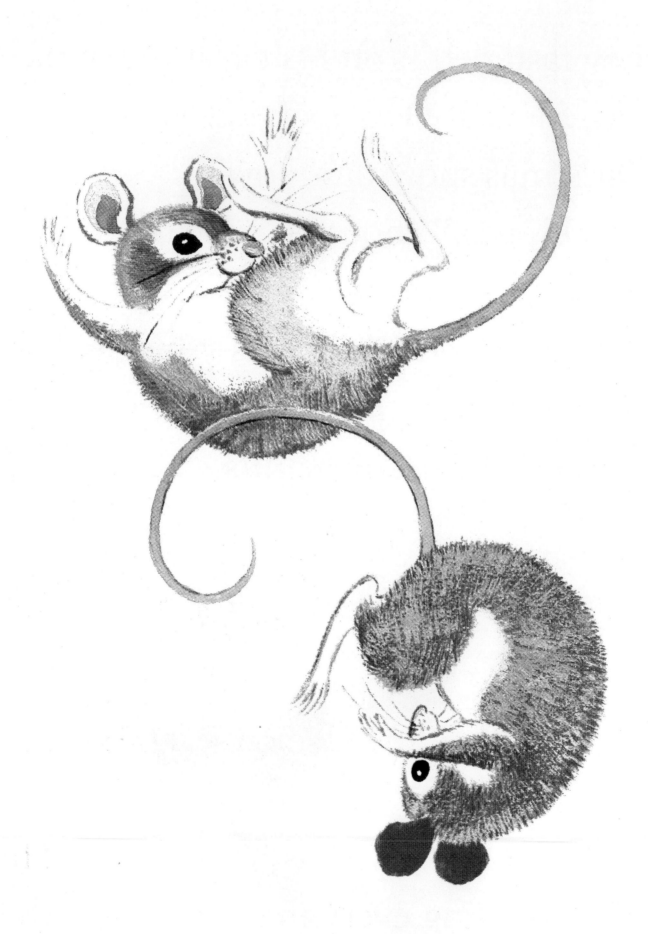

The Field Mouse children began
tumbling, too.

Sammy smiled as he watched. He
liked making everyone happy.

"*I* feel like dancing," Fanny
said. She glided around the others.
"There's just one thing. Christmas
is for everyone. The animals can
see you here, but not many people
will."

Sammy thought about it. Then
he had an idea. "Come here, Corky
Crow," he said. He whispered into
Corky's ear.

With a flap and a flutter of his wings, Corky flew off. He found some children racing downhill on their sledges. Swooping low, he grabbed a mitten someone left on the ground.

"Come back, Crow," the children
yelled. They grabbed their sledges and
followed to where the snowman stood.

"Someone decorated the snowman!" They stood admiring Sammy.
"Doesn't he make you feel good?"

said the children. "A real Christmas
snowman!" Joining hands, they
danced all around Sammy.

Up in the tree, Corky Crow danced too, clapping his wings to keep time. Squeaky Squirrel drummed on a branch with some twigs. And down below, behind a log, the Field Mouse children frolicked.

At night, when everyone slept, Sammy stood in the moonlight. He felt a lovely glow inside. His friends helped make his dream come true. He *couldn't* be happier. He was a Christmas snowman!

Noni the Christmas Reindeer

Noni could fly faster and farther
than any other reindeer at the North
Pole, but she was never allowed to
pull Santa's sleigh.

"You are too small," Santa told
her. "I need big, strong deer to haul
my heavy load. You stay at home and
guard the stable, day by day."

But it was lonely guarding the reindeer stable every day. Most of the time, Dasher, Dancer, Prancer, Vixen, Comet, Cupid, Dunder and

Blitzen were off in the fields and forests, running and jumping and getting ready for their Christmas Eve ride.

And, of course, on Christmas Eve
itself, they flew through the sky
with Santa's sack.

"Surely I can help Santa, too,"

thought Noni, one especially lonely
Christmas when even her friends,
the stable mice, had left her to sleep
together in the warm soft straw.

"If I cannot help *pull* Santa's
sleigh, then perhaps I can help
fill it!" she thought. "I will fly to
the farthest corners of the world

and find new and wonderful toys for the girls and boys."

And, on the very first day after Christmas, true to her word, off she went to the four wide ends of the earth!

"Good!" said Santa, when Noni found a little wooden clown that turned and tumbled, and stood upon his head in a hoop.

"Great!" said Santa, when she
found a tiny china chicken that
squawled and squawked and laid a
china egg.

"Grand!" said Santa, when she discovered a big silver robot—who walked and talked and stared with fiery eyes!

In the farthest nooks and crannies

of the world, Noni found more and
more wonderful toys.

"Marvellous!" said Santa, when a
queen in a faraway castle gave a
teddy bear that balanced on a string.

"Tremendous!" said Santa, when a
prince in a far-distant kingdom gave
a calico cat that swung upon a swing.

"Terrific!" cried Santa, when a king in a palace on a pinnacle gave a painted horse that pranced around a ring.

All year long, Noni found more and more toys for Santa's sack.

She found little tin trains that
puffed and whistled.

She found little tin planes that
flit and flew.

She found a fire engine with ever-

ready water, and a toy box with
ninety-five toys.

She found paints made with colours
from the rainbow, and a book brushed
with stardust and dew.

She found a flute that played tunes forever, and a crystal ball that showed the sun and moon.

Finally, on a faraway mountain in a meadow—she found a magician making dolls that danced and sang!

"Perfect!" cried Santa at last, on Christmas Eve. "But my sack is filled to overflowing, so I'll need your help to guard my heavy load."

And, almost faster than Noni could fly—he hitched her up *behind* his waiting sleigh!

"Please watch out and warn for
falling toys," he called, as he
climbed to his seat beside the sack.
Dasher, Dancer, Prancer, Vixen,

Comet, Cupid, Donner and Blitzen
flew happily at the front of Santa's
sleigh, steering their way through
the stars.

But Noni flew happily at the *back* of Santa's sleigh, watching for dolls that might tumble through the darkness, or for clowns that might topple through the clouds.

"I'll never be lonely again," she said—thinking of all the toys she would find for next Christmas, too!